Volume six of Disney Princess Classic Library

Printed in China

First Edition
1 3 5 7 9 10 8 6 4 2

F904-9088-1-12287
ISBN 978-1-4231-7947-4

For more Disney Press fun, visit www.disneybooks.com
This book was printed on paper created from a sustainable source.

Tiana and Her Loyal Friend

New York

I T WAS A BALMY AFTERNOON IN NEW ORLEANS. Big Daddy La Bouff was in the mood for some good food and good times with friends.

"Charlotte, honey!" he called out to his daughter. "How about going to Tiana's Palace for supper tonight—"

"Oh, Daddy, that would be wonderful! Just give me a minute to change."

Later, as they drove off, nobody noticed Stella the hound asleep in the back of the car!

But Stella didn't mind. In fact, the one thing that woke her up was the smell of Tiana's beignets when they reached the restaurant. Stella loved Tiana's beignets, so the hound followed her nose right into the restaurant's back kitchen.

"Big Daddy! Charlotte!" Princess Tiana warmly welcomed her friends. "Would you like to sit with my mama?"

"Why, I can't think of anyone better to share my supper with than Eudora," Big Daddy replied.

Meanwhile, Stella smelled nothing but goodness in the kitchen.

"Lookee here!" shouted one of the cooks. "We have a visitor! Here you go, puppy—have some of this gumbo. It's a new recipe!"

Stella spent a happy evening in the kitchen getting well fed and petted, while Charlotte and Big Daddy dined to Louis's jazz music and good conversation with their friends.

After the last jazz number was played, Prince Naveen's parents, the king and queen of Maldonia, got up to leave, offering Eudora a ride home.

"Why, thank you," Eudora said. Turning to Princess Tiana, she added, "I have never heard the band play quite so well as tonight. And that new gumbo—absolutely delicious. I'll see you later, sweetheart."

As everyone said their good-byes, they still didn't know about Stella . . .

. . . not until Louis entered the kitchen for his evening meal with the rest of the band.

"Grrr! Woof!" Stella was terrified of the giant alligator.

"Oh, now hold on, little dog!" Louis said to Stella. "I'm not here to eat you. I just wanted a taste of the chef's new gumbo!"

The kitchen staff backed away. They just heard growls coming from the dog and the gator.

Princess Tiana and Prince Naveen also heard the commotion as they reentered the restaurant after bidding their friends and family good night.

As soon as the prince and princess entered the kitchen, they saw a very frightened Stella plastered against a wall, barking.

"What is going on with you two?" Princess Tiana said, concerned for Stella.

"Oh, Stella," Princess Tiana said, gently petting the dog. "It's just Louis. He wouldn't hurt anybody."

"That's true!" Naveen cried as he put his arm around Louis. "Louis? He is nothing but a big guy with a bigger heart."

"Go ahead, Stella," Princess Tiana encouraged the dog. "Naveen will hold on to Louis, and you just walk right over to them."

Cautiously, Stella walked toward Louis, with Tiana by her side.

Stella sniffed Louis and then turned back toward the food. Tiana giggled. Naveen giggled. Louis wanted to giggle, but he thought he might scare Stella all over again.

It didn't take long for the staff of Tiana's Palace to put together a supper made up of that evening's leftovers. Prince Naveen played the ukulele, and Tiana made some of her special beignets—just for Stella.

Before dawn, the prince and princess dropped Stella off at the La Bouff estate. No one had even noticed she was missing yet!

"Good night, Stella," Princess Tiana said, giving the dog a big hug. "And don't be a stranger. When I stop by, I expect you to come out and get your own beignets."

Stella gave one last woof and went toward the house. She'd had the best night of her life.